Between the Notched Pines

Hunter Nichols

Goose River Press
Waldoboro, Maine

Library of Congress Card Number: 2020952726

ISBN: 978-1-59713-229-9

First Printing, 2021

Cover photo by Hunter Nichols.

Published by
Goose River Press
3400 Friendship Road
Waldoboro ME 04572
e-mail: gooseriverpress@roadrunner.com
www.gooseriverpress.com

For Fathers

and Sons

of New England

Chapter 1

Peter Hennessey lived to the ripe old age of eighty-five before passing comfortably in his sleep from natural causes. He was found in his bed by his nursing aid that visited in the mornings and evenings. His wife of sixty years had gone just a year before him. Peter had enjoyed his life, sharing his passion for the great outdoors as often as he could with his family. A true Mainer, he taught his two sons to fish not long after they could walk, and his adoring wife always supported their trips to the river. She knew that Peter would keep everyone safe and that they would come home with bellies full of trout. He had a sense of humor and levity that not every one of his generation was blessed with. Little bothered him as he seemed to survey each day for the bigger picture. He was physically strong, with broad shoulders and big calloused hands. He was spiritually strong too with unwavering love for his dear wife Delores who he affectionately called "DeDe," and in his love for his family.

Peter didn't leave behind much money but he didn't leave any debt either. In his will he left his house to his two sons who decided to rent it out to a family from town and split the money. To his granddaughters, a few thousand dollars each; they were in college and he thought it best to let them figure out how to use the money. To his only grandson he left a letter.

Connor Hennessey, Peter's grandson, had received the sad news days earlier but waited to open the letter. He had been busy, going into work early and leaving late. His company was on the brink of merging with a larger organization and he was one of the few people with the savvy to facilitate a smooth transition. Work had consumed him for the past several years and he hadn't gotten to see his aging grandfather outside of a few family holiday gatherings. The letter was a painful reminder of that; although, that was not its intention. Connor felt guilty for not seeing his grandfather more in his later years. They had been so close when he was a kid, even up through high school and college. When Peter had a hard time joining Connor and his father fishing, Connor would still take him to breakfast on Sunday mornings and tell him all about it: what they caught, how many, the weather, the campfire, how thick the blackflies or mosquitos were, anything and everything. He had seen him only once since the passing of his grandmother and that was for a rather somber Christmas dinner.

It was past eight o'clock on a Wednesday night and Connor had come home early from an afterwork gathering to fire off a few emails while the rest of his colleagues enjoyed cold beers at the bar. He looked at the small, black kitchen table he had in his one-bedroom apartment and fixed upon the white envelope containing the unopened letter. Connor walked to the refrigerator, grabbed a Harpoon IPA, and popped the top with the bottle opener on his keys. Flipping the cap into the trash can, he sat down at the kitchen table. With a gulp of courage, he opened the letter.

Hey Bub,

If you are reading this then you know it was my time. Hopefully I'm playing cards with your grandmother like we used to do on Friday nights when you were all just kids. I know life has gotten very busy for you, and everyone is proud of the career you have made for yourself down in the city. You are my only grandson and the memories I have of the two of us together are some of the happiest of my life. Your grandmother always used to talk about how you would light up the room when you came in with your little fishing pole, ready to head to the brook with your father and me. Thinking of her makes me think of you and what a happy kid you always were, no matter how many we caught! As this letter is part of my will you may be wondering what I have left you. I left the house to your father and uncle...what the hell would you want with that old house anyway? I didn't have a lot of money but what cash I had I gave to the girls. They are in school, so I figure they can use it more than you. For you, my favorite grandson, I leave you with a task. Do you remember our old fishing camp way Downeast? Yes sir, that's the one. I know you are picturing it in your head now. I hope you remember how to get in there, I'm sure your father can show you the access road on a map if you've forgotten. My final wish is for you to go there. Now since I am updating this letter after your grandmother passed, I do not know when you will be receiving it. If it's the winter don't be a knucklehead and snowshoe in there, you'll freeze to death! Wait until the spring, after the cold spring waters recede. Best time for trout anyway, right? I know you have said that job you have is busy and tough to get away from, but this is my last wish, so you get your ass up there! The key is in the same place as it always was. You remember, don't you? There's a reason for all this, I promise. But like anything in this life, you are going to have to work for it. Stay on the trail after the road, follow the river, and keep it between the notched pines.

Love you always,

Papa Peter

With a tear in his eye Connor folded up the letter and stuffed it in his pants pocket. He truly had a special bond with his grandfather and if this was his last wish he knew he had to do it. In a momentary flash he remembered driving down the dirt roads on the way to camp, Papa Peter repeatedly banging his knee with the floor stick shift in his old F-150 as he sat in the middle of the bench seat. He remembered the smell of the truck and of his grandfather's flannel shirt: woodsmoke with a hint of tobacco from when he used to smoke a cigar now and again on the river. *Keeps the bugs away,* he would always say, then wait a second and say with a wink and smile, *and your grandmother won't let me do it at home.* He also remembered the old black lab Eddie that used to ride down with them. He loved that dog. Eddie was part of the family, and in the early days Connor would run around the camp with him after they had gotten back from fishing until it was time to eat.

The problem now was how to get the time. Heading from Boston to Maine was a trip itself but then to go

Downeast and hike through the woods to the old camp would take days that he didn't have with the merger looming.

"Mr. Tannehill, it's Connor. Sorry to call you after nine but I need a minute of your time, sir," Connor said dialing up his boss Lennie.

"What is it? What have you heard?" his boss asked nervously. The future of the company depended on this deal going through and although Connor wasn't in charge, he was a key member of the young software company despite being just twenty-seven years of age.

"Nothing, it's nothing like that. I have a family issue. I need a few days to get up to Maine. My grandfather passed, do you remember me saying so a few days ago?" Connor asked.

"Oh, yes. Sorry again about that Con, I remember you saying you were close. I thought you said he was cremated, and it was just a small gathering. We worked right through last weekend, I'm sorry you didn't get to go up." Lennie apologized while still managing to pry.

Connor thought for a second: *Did I really say that? Did I really skip my own grandfather's wake because of company business?*

He felt even more guilty and now uneasy about sharing so many details. He hadn't hardly even talked to his own father about the passing. They had spoken on the phone for a few minutes, Connor offered his condolences; he was, of course, upset, but he didn't take the time to be there for his father and to remember what his grandfather had meant to both of them until right at that moment, in the middle of a phone call with his anxious boss.

"Con? You there, kid?" Lennie asked.

5

"Hey, yes, I'm still here, lost myself there for a minute," Connor said, regaining control of his emotions enough to speak up into the receiver. "I really need the rest of the week off," Connor insisted, his tone quiet but serious.

"I don't understand, the wake was last weekend. The merger...I need you, Connor. You are on the rise in this company." His boss did not understand. In one sentence, as only bosses can do, he stroked his ego and gave a gentle warning. "Let's sleep on it, I know you want to see your family and all, I get it, but they will still be up in New Hampshire next weekend, won't they? Hit the hay kid, I'll see you bright and early at the office, we can talk about how we are going to finalize these proposals and close this thing up." His boss hung up the phone.

Even though Mr. Tannehill was an asshole, Connor couldn't help but give him one hundred and ten percent. He had been with the company for five years. One was an intern year where he didn't even get paid and had to work a second job to cover living expenses. He was wired for hard work, inculcated from a young age to have pride in his approach to school and work. Connor saw opportunity in a challenge, even to a fault. His boss was perceptive and used this to work Connor tirelessly. From time to time he would become frustrated, but he always soldiered on.

Connor sat at his small kitchen table looking around his apartment. It was nice for a guy his age. The place was spotless and organized with sleek, modern furniture. His sixty-inch TV remained off since he had come in. All his pictures hung in black, metal frames that balanced sharply with the unblemished walls.

Glancing over them he noticed one of him white water rafting from early college with a group of friends. Another picture was a hiking trip he used to go on every year with a bunch of high school buddies; he hadn't talked to them in five years. In the pictures Connor looked stocky and strong as he always did, but his eyes were kind and his smile wide as he goofed off with his pals. His frame hadn't changed much but that smile was often wiped away and replaced with a more shrewd, focused look. His flashing blue eyes were now hidden under a furrowed brow as he lived day-to-day in a fraught company matrix. His once shaggy light-brown hair was neatly trimmed and invariable. His clean-shaven face appeared pastier than in the photos where he had been out in the sun. His attire almost entirely switched from flannels and blue jeans to slacks and button downs even when he wasn't at the office. He continued to scan the wall and came to a picture of himself and his father in a canoe, all geared up, his father smiling and a twelve-year old Connor holding up a fish that you couldn't quite make out in the old photo. Connor realized he had begun to lose himself. He hadn't been out with someone that wasn't from work in months. His boss knew more about his family happenings than anyone else he talked to. Frustrated, Connor sat down on his couch and turned on the Red Sox game to try and clear his head. It was the top half of the sixth inning and baseball brought him right back to thinking about his family. Connor, his father, and Papa Peter all loved listening to baseball on the radio, which was good because Downeast at the camp it was the only station that would come in. They used to listen to day games on the river and night games at the camp after getting a fire going. Connor opened another beer and pulled the letter back out of his pocket. He read it again and could hear his grandfather's voice. He began to tear up and thought of his father. It was too late to call, and he didn't know what he might say anyway. Things had not been the same between them in recent years. Instead, he watched the Red Sox and had another beer.

That night he laid in bed. After a twelve-hour work day, an emotional evening, and the better part of a six pack of IPAs, he was sure he would sleep soundly, but he didn't. Thoughts of his family ran through his head. Then he wondered about those boys from the rafting picture and then about his high school buddies. He even thought about the girl he dated after college, she was a keeper but didn't fit in with his "me first" agenda. No one did.

Chapter 2

The alarm went off at six and Connor rose, still tired from his restless night, but like a good worker-bee he caffeinated and headed for the office. After lumbering down the stairs of his old brick apartment building and back up the concrete steps to street level he saw his bus pull up to the stop. At a dead sprint he was able to slide his hand in before the doors closed. He tapped his pass to pay the fare and surveyed the sea of people stuffed into the bus. No seats available, no eye contact. The bus was already packed at six-thirty in the morning, so he stood holding the floor to ceiling metal bar that was almost certainly used as a crutch for a drunkard the night before. The bus had the slight smell of urine and body odor. An unwashed man leaned too close to him and mumbled something about God, the devil, and the president. The combination of lurching forward and screeching to a halt every few seconds plus the IPAs made him start to sweat. After seven or eight stops he got off the bus halfway and walked the remainder of the commute to get some air. Connor took a deep breath of the spring morning, which was of fresh mulch from recently planted trees mixed with exhaust fumes from the busy street. At the same moment a suit stepped from a coffee shop onto the curb. Lighting a cigarette, he exhaled almost directly at Connor, blowing smoke without any attempt to redirect it. Two people rushed past him on either side, one bumping his shoulder in the process and continuing without looking back. He truly loved the city but, however lively and interesting it could be, there was an element that felt confining and inescapable. Some days the beautiful stone sculptures, historic landmarks, old neighborhoods, and intricate facades and masonry could be appreciated. But other days he felt imprisoned by concrete, rebar, and sky scrapers that ran to the edge of the street. The influx of new buildings and people seemed to be without end and he often felt bombarded by the chaos. But this was the path he chose and most of the time he reassured himself it was right. Sometimes he would go in on a Sunday morning as much to advance on work as for the juxtaposition of pace.

Standing on the curb awaiting the walk signal with the masses, he straightened out. His head began to clear, and work entered his mind. He made his way through the crowds and over the steaming manhole covers into the downtown office. Connor was always one of the first people there. Immediately he felt back in his element and got right down to business. His bulleted proposal for integrating company software and workflow to accommodate the merger was complete by the time his boss arrived at a quarter to nine. He then proceeded to work on the presentation that was scheduled for the following week, which of course his boss needed by Friday.

Working unremittingly in his cubicle and powering down another cup of coffee Connor continued to produce, now working on the slide deck for a different presentation he would create but ultimately not present. When he reached into his pocket to grab his USB and save his work, he felt something: the letter. He thought that the beers must have gotten to him a little because he realized he was wearing the same dress pants from the evening before when he folded it into his pocket. Connor resisted reading it again and stuffed it back behind his wallet, but now it was on his mind. All the feelings he had the night before came racing back. He tried to block them out, to focus on work. He knew it was important and that he was positioning himself well in the company. Surely, he didn't love what he did for work, but he wanted to continue to push for more. It's what he was supposed to do. Pouring sixty-five hours a week into this company had to be worth something eventually. The emails, the early meetings, the stress, and being constantly tethered to work had to pay off. But the thought of going against a Last Will and Testament, of breaking a bond with his dead grandfather, forced him to grapple with his conscience.

"Connor, good to see you here working hard this morning!" Lennie said, standing over Connor with a cup of coffee in his hand. "How is everything coming along, son? Going to need your work soon...I won't be in this Saturday, so I'll have a look before I take off for the long weekend." His paunchy boss was notorious for asking a question that he always seemed to deem rhetorical before making his demands. Lennie stared down at Connor while nonchalantly pursing his lips and adjusting his tie, as if that would help it realign with the protruding buttons. His mind was comfortable giving orders, but his body always appeared a little uncomfortable as he regularly readjusted himself and dabbed sweat from his thinning hairline.

"Everything is coming along well, sir. You aren't staying here this weekend to oversee the work ahead of the big meeting next week?" Connor asked, somewhat surprised to hear what sounded like a weekend on Cape Cod. He knew Lennie had a nice place in Hyannis and liked to go down there as often as possible.

"No, I'll be overseeing from my place on the water this weekend, but your work I will need to see as soon as possible. I still need you around this weekend, so no running off to Vermont. Okay, Con?" Lennie asked with his patented rhetoric, as he strolled off to the next cubicle, ruining weekends and raising stress one step at a time.

Connor sat in the no-man's-land of cubicles between the closed doors on either side of the sprawling office floor. He looked around as others attempted to appear busy, shuffling papers and organizing file cabinets while waiting for their turn in the fire. He contemplated everything from his current role in the company to his boss's false sense of security in the office. He knew he was a mess underneath and only wanted to run off to his fancy house to hide for the weekend. Connor thought long and hard about what to do next. For the last few years work had been everything to him, but before that the most important thing was family and that meant Peter Hennessey: a true patriarch if there ever was one. If he made this his final request there had to be a reason for it.

"Lennie," Connor said, briskly and confidently strolling into his office, "here is all my finished work ahead of schedule for next week. Everything is there."

Connor dropped the paperwork on his boss's desk followed by a USB on top of the manila folders. He realized he had never really stormed into the boss's office, in fact he was not sure if he had ever even called him by his first name; usually it was sir, boss, or Mr. Tannehill. His confidence grew. "I am not going to Vermont, or to New Hampshire. I'll be in Maine taking care of some important family business. I'll be back ahead of the meeting next week." Connor turned and walked out of the office without Lennie saying a word. He wasn't sure if this was a good or bad thing, but he knew his work was solid, so his job security was probably still intact. Even his sly tyrant of a boss could not fire someone for bereavement on his way out. He looked up at the calendar on the wall of his cubicle. It was June 1st: the river was prime.

Chapter 3

The tumultuous morning was over, but Connor still wrestled with the gravitational pull toward work. He rarely drove as that meant leaving the city and the office behind. He sat stiffly in the cloth seat of his 2009 Toyota Camry, white-knuckling the steering wheel with clinched sweaty hands. This was not out of necessity for adherence to the road but as a sort of stress reliever that was not very effective. His mind raced 100 mph while his sensible automobile stood still until able to crawl forward by a few rotations of the tires. He grinded down Storrow Drive on his way to Route 1; it was there that he planned to meet up with Interstate 95 North and trek another 250 miles straight ahead into the state of Maine. It was a hot day for early June and the sun shone down brightly on the car with scarcely a cloud in the sky. Connor day dreamed of floating down stream with a soft breeze blowing in his face. He was quickly jolted back to reality by a car horn and break lights just ahead of him. It was already three o'clock and he knew he would be sitting in traffic for what would seem like an eternity.

Gotta get outta the rat race bub, can't catch no fish in a cubicle. Connor could hear his grandfather's words echoing in his head.

He strained forward to see through the sun and traffic. Beads of sweat fell from his brow onto his white dress shirt and solid black tie as he revisited his office rebellion. He wondered if this would cost him and if he was just on an eternal path to more responsibility without opportunity. He already worked more hours than anyone else there, churned through project after project, and didn't knock off early or take sick days. Despite all the early arrivals and late departures, extra hours and effort, the only moves he seemed to make were lateral. Connor could still hear the sentiment of his boss: "If you want to get ahead in this company you must 'Prioritize!'" This was one of his favorite opening lines to boom off the conference room walls. It was usually followed by a vague tirade about this or that until he felt he had applied a sufficient amount of pressure onto his employees. Connor allowed himself a quick smile when he thought about how his change in "priorities" today made Lennie feel at the moment.

After a nauseating ninety-minute stretch which had him wondering when he last got new brake pads, Connor finally hit the interstate. With moderate traffic there were tail lights as far as the eye could see but they were moving at near-normal highway speeds. The blur of lights and bumpers further gave way to open road after reaching the New Hampshire border. Connor climbed with the highway to the green, metal bridge carrying him over the Piscataquis River into Maine. He maneuvered past all the out-of-state plates slowing down to exit in Wells, Ogunquit, and Kennebunk. Taking I-295 North and driving through Portland he felt the temperature change; the ocean had made the air cooler and more comfortable. The previously hot sun turned pleasant and the cool air was refreshing. His phone buzzed, rattling around in the cup holder. It had to be another work email from colleagues on the project; at this point it couldn't be anything else. The unyielding barrage of work emails was nearly impossible to turn off. In the brief Portland traffic he was able to shoot off replies here and there. Responses that would fend off the wolves, at least for now. Nonetheless, he was beyond the constraints of his cubicle and had more important matters to attend to. Getting closer to home he began to relax and stopped thinking about work almost completely.

Work will be right there when you get back, Connor could again hear his grandfather's words of wisdom. This time they were words to his father, who suffered from a similar workaholism when Connor was a boy. His father did make time to go fishing, even if he was wringing his hands and thinking about his business for the first hour of the trip. But with the help of a few Bud tall boys he would eventually relax, and usually down a few more thereafter.

Increasingly comfortable now in a familiar setting, Connor rolled the window down. The wind flowed between his fingers and his right wrist rested atop the steering wheel, lazily guiding the car north. The farther he went the fewer cars were on the road and the denser the green forest was on either side of the interstate. The distance between exits grew and the scenery between was of constant thick forest broken only by rivers running underneath the highway and a small town here and there. Eventually, Connor reached his exit to turn off the highway. He hadn't noticed that the radio station he was listening to had been completely lost, and mindlessly he twisted the dial to turn the radio off as he cruised onward. He drove past the town gas station and the little cafe that was sure to be busy on Sunday mornings. A Little League baseball game had just finished and the kids were all eating ice cream at the snack shack. With the window down, a soft breeze blew the smell of fresh cut grass from the baseball diamond into the car. Connor remembered playing there as a kid, his father Walt coaching the team just as Papa Peter had coached Walt when he was a boy. Peter always brought peanuts for Connor and the kids to have in the dugouts; no one was allergic to nuts back then. During practice, a focused Walt relentlessly hammered ground balls and pop flies at his players. Walt was shorter and a little smaller than Peter but strong as a bull and had the energy to work all day and coach the kids nearly every night of the week. He was a hard-ass of a coach even then and that would only get more true as time went on.

While reliving some of those childhood days, Connor coasted to his parents' new home on Elm Street. It was a little white ranch with grey shutters, flower boxes under the windows, a neatly trimmed yard, an American flag waving slightly in the breeze, and was just a mile from his old house. He and his friends had played ball, rode bikes, and got into mischief all around the old neighborhood. Good memories were rushing back as he navigated the streets at neighborhood speeds. However, he also remembered being in high school and chomping at the bit to move on to the next chapter of his life, as nearly all adolescents tend to do. Back now for the first time in a while, Connor waved to a few neighbors that seemed not to fully recognize him, and finally pulled into the driveway behind his mother's car.

Chapter 4

"Connor!" His mother exclaimed, "You're home! I had no idea you were coming, I would have cooked something fresh. What brought you up here? Is everything all right?" Anita, Connor's mother, asked in a relative state of disbelief as she trotted down the driveway toward him. She worked through her range of emotions from excited parent to concerned mother in a matter of moments. She looked exactly the same as the last time he had seen her except for a couple more gray strands in her brown hair. She was always petite and fit and still had the spring in her step as she bounded toward her son.

"Hey Mom! I'm doing well, everything is all right," Connor replied, his smile giving confirmation to his words as he walked up the driveway with open arms.

"I am so happy to see you! It's been a while. Do we have you for a few days? I can call your sisters and see if they want to come down for dinner tomorrow night?" Anita asked, jumping right into family mode. She was always trying to get everyone together. A family meal gave her a sense of pride and tradition. Just the thought brought her back to a happier time when all the kids were running around the backyard. She would call out through the screen door off the porch that dinner was ready, and they would come rushing inside to eat a home-cooked meal. Anita would make everyone get up and wash their hands with a gentle scolding that brought them smiling back to the table. Her mind drifted to that place even though it had long since passed.

Connor brought her back from her blissful reverie as he followed her inside. "I don't think there will be time for a family gathering this go around. I am just here for the night. Papa Peter left me a letter in his will, and I needed to come home to fulfill his wishes. I'm heading to the river first thing in the morning. You remember our old camp Downeast?" Connor asked.

"Of course, how could I forget the boys club? Between you, your father, and Grandpa Peter someone was always pushing to go there," she recalled, letting the thought of everyone back together ease out of her mind.

"If you do talk to the girls tell them I said hello, maybe I can see them sometime this summer, or maybe fall would be better," Connor said, working through the reality of how rarely he could return home.

"I'm sure they would appreciate a call from their brother..." Anita replied, trailing off as she turned towards the counter with her disapproving tone setting in.

"I know I have been a bit distant. I'm sorry I wasn't here for the wake," Connor solemnly answered. Tightening his lips, he looked down and scuffed the bottom of his shoe on the tile floor as Anita turned her gaze back on him. His obvious disappointment in himself was enough and she did not press further but stayed on the topic.

"Your father has been having a bit of a tough time.

You know how close they were and how it was you that kept them so connected all those years. When you left they didn't spend as much time together. I think it has weighed heavily on him but, of course he doesn't want to talk about it. You know how he is," she sighed.

"I didn't leave, I went to college and got a job. And yes, I do know how he is," Connor softly defended, trying to be more level-headed than he had been during previous visits home.

"I know, I know, I didn't mean it like that," she offered, trying to smooth the tension. "It's just been a rough stretch around here. Your father is away on business but is set to come home tomorrow. It would mean a lot for you to see him. I realize things haven't been very good between you two, but he just always wants the best for you," his mother said. She was not the type of person to use guilt as a weapon. Anita was a wonderful mother and wife and a rock for the family. In times when Connor and his father didn't see eye to eye, which became more frequent as he got older, she was able to diffuse those situations tactfully. In the early days, Connor and his father often ended up in front of the TV watching the Sox and talking about a river or lake they wanted to get out on together. But as time went on, the two butted heads harder than ever, like a couple of old rams, and even Anita-the-fixer couldn't always get through to them.

"I would love to see Walt, it's been a while now. I'm going to head to the river in the morning but hopefully I can catch him on the way back through," Connor said, staying his planned course. He did want to see his father but wasn't sure how. He also thought it possible his father may come home and need to *head back to the*

21

office which he tended to do when bothered by something. That was a line for the kids. Anita knew that meant the Elks Lodge, but she didn't make a fuss about it. Walt always came home eventually, even if he took a zig-zag route down the sidewalk.

Sitting on stools in the kitchen and sharing one of his father's beers, Anita and Connor had a chance to catch up. She told him all about his sisters and how they were doing great in college, making friends, and having fun. Anita and the girls were very close, like Walt and Connor used to be. Anita asked Connor about work for which he had a prepared answer to suggest everything was all right. As for questions about friends and girls he remained vague. It was almost obvious that he couldn't be holding anything back as there truly wasn't much to divulge. Anita sensed that and she knew better than to pry. She hugged her son and told him to make sure he smelled the roses once in a while.

"All right, well there is left over Shepard's Pie in the fridge. I love you, but I need to get ready for bed. Have a safe trip down to the river, all your gear should be right where you left it in the garage," Anita said, drifting toward the stairs.

"Thanks," Connor smiled.

"Don't forget to take a flashlight and there's a first aid kit under your father's work bench. Remember you won't have cell service once you get way down on the Airline." Anita knew Connor could handle himself. He learned how to fish, read maps, hike, and navigate terrain at a young age with Walt and Peter but it was still her job to worry, she couldn't help it.

"Thanks, Mom. I haven't been away *that* long," Connor joked. "I will take some of that Shepard's Pie

though, and maybe just one more of Walt's beers."
Connor still often called his father by his first name,
Walter. After too many talks where his father repeatedly
told him he needed to *act like a man* he adopted this
habit as a way of doing so and it stuck.
Anita and Connor shared their goodnights. Connor
sat on his perch at the kitchen counter with a heaping
plate of Shepard's Pie and a cold pale ale from a local
brewery. He did like Walt's choice of beer. After nearly
inhaling a home-cooked meal, Connor began to take in
the new house. It was a downsize from the one he had
grown up in. He had of course been to the new house
several times, but he finally began to look around. The
house was clean and neat with everything perfectly
organized, thanks to Anita. Walking along the wall in
the living room he noticed the photos of his sisters
playing soccer and softball, their pigtails and braces
made him smile as he thought of them running around
the old house. Now they were both in college at the
University of Maine Orono. He missed them and knew
he had dropped the ball a bit on keeping in contact. He
then saw a picture of himself holding a trophy, his
father behind him with the coach's clipboard. That was
from the Babe Ruth League, and they both looked
happy and proud. Next, he saw a picture of his grandparents, which appeared to have been recently dusted
and handled. It was of the two of them on top of Mount
Battie down on the coast in Camden. It became their
favorite place to stay as they got older. They would go
for long walks together in the state park and visit the
peak of Mount Battie to overlook Camden Harbor and
beyond into the bay. Looking at the photos, the rush of
contrasting emotions returned. He felt sadness for the

loss of his grandparents, but joy for the time they had together. He also felt guilt for not being there for his father and anger toward him for their fractured relationship. He looked away from the pictures on the wall and took a deep breath. Exhaling, he finished Walt's beer and realized he was tremendously tired. Connor sat down and within five minutes, he was asleep on the couch. It had been a long day, and finally at home, even a new home, he slept soundly.

Chapter 5

In the morning Connor awoke to birds chirping and the sun coming through the light summer curtains. The window was ajar, and the breeze of cool spring air was chilly and invigorating. Refreshed and excited, as one is early in the morning when not confined to a cubicle, Connor popped off the couch, flipped the switch on the coffee pot, and prepared for his trip Downeast. He didn't worry about a shower, this was as clean as he would likely be for the next few days. He could hear his grandfather's words echoing in his mind again, *Don't worry about having a little lather on ya, it'll help keep the flies off.* Of course, that probably wasn't true, but it always made everyone feel better about not showering.

After dressing quickly, Connor chugged a cup of coffee and scarfed down a chocolate sugared Mrs. Dunster's donut, a staple of the Hennessey clan, then hit the garage. He found his rod and tackle box right where he had left them next to his father's and the spare that they always brought and left back in the truck. Grabbing the essential items, he also checked his flashlight, and took the first aid kit, upon his mother's request. He didn't figure he'd need it, but the Maine woods should not be underestimated. He piled everything in the back seat of his car and poked his head back in the house, he wanted to say goodbye to his mother, but she was still asleep. It was 6:15 a.m.

Jumping into his faithful Camry he headed east toward Bangor. His excitement grew as he sailed past the few cars on the road at that time of day. Getting to Bangor, he took I-395 to Route 1A, headed east, then skipped over to Route 9, or as Mainers call it: The Airline. There are a few common reasons why this stretch of state Route 9 from Bangor to Calais is thought to be called the Airline. One is that it's named after the Airline Staging Company, which used to deliver both mail and passengers by horse drawn carriage through the 1850's and beyond. Another is that this route was shorter than the coastal route and therefore called the Airline in reference to being a shortcut.

Now things began to feel like the old days: flying along the Airline without any traffic, coming into and quickly out of tiny towns, each complete with a church and a country store. Some with a few gas pumps, a small school, and a town hall. The space between towns seemed to grow the farther east he went. Driving down the two-lane highway, he absorbed the tall, beautiful, green pines stretching into the sky, the jagged rock formations rising and falling, and the occasional stream passing under the winding road, which often flowed to a nearby lake or pond. He was so preoccupied with the eastward journey he forgot to look at his phone until he got past Aurora and by that time the cellphone service was long gone. When Connor got to the Airline Snack Bar, which was just another country store that also made pretty good snacks, he pulled in. Grabbing a gallon of water and a bag of ice for the cooler, he stocked his soft cooler with three cartons of nightcrawlers, a small tub of butter, two fresh house-made Italian sandwiches, beef jerky, mixed nuts, and a two-liter bottle of ginger ale to go with the handle of whiskey he had swiped from Walt's cabinet. He had hoped the cabin was still supplied with some of the non-perishable items it always had in the past, but with no way of knowing, he figured it safer to get some water in case the pots and pans were ruined, or he couldn't get a fire going. Then, after gassing up, he set off down Route 193 toward the blueberry barrens.

Turning off the Airline, the road became more narrow. A tight two-lane stretch full of dips and dives, with trees on either side of the ditches, and a crumbling shoulder that gave way to sandy gravel beside the road. He had driven it so many times he remembered where to speed up to get that little rise over a hump in the road, which still gave his stomach a fun kind of flip-flop. And he remembered where to slow down to avoid rolling into the ditch. The narrow road eventually leads to an opening and the trees fan out to display the fields of blueberry bushes that always seem endless. The road flattens with the land and the blueberry barrens are as far as the eye can see on either side.

For the next leg of the journey, Connor recalled the importance of choosing the correct dirt road to turn onto. There are approximately one hundred of these dirt roads all leading out into the everlasting blueberry bushes that were mostly green now but would be bursting blue with berries in August. He passed a few fields that had been spot burned painting a portion of the undulating land cranberry red for now, but that in the future would produce a plentiful harvest. As he drove he carefully contemplated the options. Braking and peering through the dusty window he suddenly remembered the way. He took a left and slowed down considerably to avoid blowing out a tire on the grated gravel. He heard a thump under the car and then felt another under his feet, and at that moment he realized he should own a truck. His car was the sensible option for city life but not so sensible out here. Continuing to creep along, he tried to avoid the potholes and rolled up his windows each time he saw the stacks of boxes he knew contained thousands of honey bees. They wouldn't cause him any trouble, but better safe than stung.

Connor began to smile when he came to a fork in the road, he became reassured that he had guessed correctly. He branched right onto another narrow dirt road, this one less maintained and much tighter with the wild blueberries coming right up to the edge of it. Approaching a group of pines that seemed to be a dividing line in the bush he took an immediate left. This turn was crucial because what was previously one hundred dirt roads at the main drag turns into what seems like a million tiny offshoots. Once this far in country you only see people occasionally and usually when they are harvesting the berries or tending to the bees. Now the road was so tight that if someone was approaching, backing out would be the only option. But in all the times down this way that had only happened once or twice. Suddenly, Connor remembered getting lost down one of these roads in his teenage years, after all they really do all look the same; dirt roads in an ocean of blueberries with beehive islands. When he got turned around it was late summer, and he had been out raking berries. He could hear his grandfather guiding him again, *Trace back the way you came in, use the pines, and if you get stumped, pull out the 'Gazetteer.'* Connor smiled as he thought of his father and grandfather showing him how to use the coveted *Maine Gazetteer* on different trips up North. Use of the *Gazetteer* is a rite of passage for any outdoorsman in Maine as it contains a set of maps showing roads and access points to the rivers, lakes, and mountains of Maine. His father would always tell him: "It's best to learn how to use the *Gazetteer* because where we are headed technology won't help you."

The road began to dip downward and to the right toward the tree line with big rocks on either side. It got darker and more wet indicating to Connor that he was close. He pulled up into a clearing to the right off the road, which was now more of a trail than anything for cars. Going any farther in a Camry would not be wise. Without cell service getting a tow would not be a viable option if he were to get stuck. He turned the car off, opened the door, and heard the river a hundred yards away; he had made it.

Chapter 6

The path down toward the river was muddy from recent heavy rain. Connor could hear the river easily; it sounded louder than he remembered. He was excited. Before saddling up his gear he sprayed himself down with Ben's 100% DEET repellent, a favorite of all those who have spent time battling mosquitos and blackflies in the Maine woods. Connor looked a little more like the pictures in his apartment now with his dry-fit pants, blue flannel shirt, baseball hat and sunglasses atop his head. He headed down toward the rushing river with his rod in one hand, tackle box in the other, a cooler strapped across his chest, and a pack of essentials on his back. On the right of the road sat two towering pines. Each scarred with small notches cut with a hatchet, this marked the trail. *Keep it between the notched pines,* he could hear his grandfather saying. *That will bring you right out to your father and me.*

Connor worked his way down the path. It was a little overgrown as it hadn't been cleared in a few years, but he knew where he was going. Following the sound of the river on his left he walked parallel to it for a few hundred yards before coming to a second set of pines. He remembered, even without looking, where they had been notched or scarred. To him they resembled a doorway into the wilderness that he so loved. He kept on walking, skillfully ducking tree branches, stepping over thick shrubbery and downed trees and shaking off spiderwebs. Connor kept his fishing pole, a four-and-a-half-foot ultralight Ugly Stik rod, that was tailor made for these tight and woodsy conditions, pointed straight to avoid entanglement as the trail grew thicker.

Keeping the water as his guide on the left, he came into a clearing of waist high bushes and tall thin wisps and he could see down to the river. For a brief fifty yards or so the river flattened, the banks weren't so steep, and the water appeared a little more shallow. With this the sound of the quick, cold, spring water quieted to a trickle.

Coming out of the forest and able to see the waterway for the first time he stopped for a moment to take in the scenery. His focus had been on the trail, staying locked in on what was directly ahead of him to avoid snapping his rod on a tree or ending up with a face full of spiders. In the clearing Connor took a deep breath and exhaled. As he looked at the majestic river he felt at peace. A few flowers sprouted up to his right along the tree line, but he couldn't say what they were if his life depended on it. Knowledge of flowers, he thought, was one thing not passed down to him. Stretching his back, he looked behind him to the thick woods, unable to hear anything but the trickle of the quelled brook and a few birds chirping. From this vantage point the mid-morning sun was well over the treetops.

Connor turned his attention back toward the flattened water when to the right in his periphery he saw something move. Suddenly, his heart leapt. He took a quick, short breath, and jolted back a half step before

31

realizing what it was. A large bull moose stood in the middle of the shallow part of the river. He wasn't easily spotted before as he was downstream and previously very still. Despite only being in the clearing for a few seconds, Connor was still mildly shocked he hadn't spotted the big bull right away. He immediately relaxed knowing this mammoth creature was simply cooling down in the boggy conditions created by the shallows. Being in the water gave access to vegetation from over-hanging trees and was a natural barrier to keep the flies off while trying to get cool. Connor stopped for a few minutes to watch him. When the moose turned his head his beautiful set of antlers became visible. They must have been nearly four feet across and quite thick. He had some grass or lily pads tangled on them, and as he moved his massive head they dripped back into the water. Of course, Connor knew these animals could be dangerous, but only if you were in their way. Staying a safe distance, he watched the moose wallow in the river and then continued his journey back into the woods on the other side of the clearing.

Keeping the river within earshot on his left, Connor made his way another quarter mile down the rugged path into a second clearing. Here he could see the roof of the old fishing camp. His heart began to race again, although not as much as being embarrassingly startled by the moose. *Only a city boy would get all stirred up by a moose cooling off in the river,* his grandfather's voice poked fun at him in his mind, which brought a little smile to his face. It was a good reminder for him to be more aware. These woods were always kind to him but there could be treachery at any turn, especially being out there alone. The animals were one thing, but the elements and the thick forest always presented another challenge entirely. He remembered the time they were caught in a thunderstorm on Ragged Lake, their aluminum boat being tossed about as sheets of rain poured down. His grandfather looked over at him and said: *If you don't like the weather, wait five minutes.* Of course, that was the saying of many old Mainers. On that day, everyone enjoyed the weather until time stood still as thunder, lightning, and whitecaps threatened their fourteen-foot vessel.

Connor, a child at the time, remembered being scared to death, but his grandfather cranked them to shore while his father held on to young Connor. That became an early lesson in staying calm and understanding that a situation can change quickly.

Approaching the cabin, Connor could see no one had been there in some time, likely not since the previous summer. The grass had begun to shoot up around the camp and spiderwebs were in every corner, even in front of the doorway to get in. The branch of a birch tree had split and fallen on the roof but didn't appear to have caused serious damage. He pulled the birch branch off and used it to wipe the spiderwebs away from the door frame before casting it back into the woods. He could hear the river rushing even when back in the woods; it was less than forty yards away. Walking to the edge of the camp Connor reached up to the bottom most part of the overhanging roof. Behind the edge there was an empty space. Connor slid his hand back there and immediately felt the jar he was looking for. It was an old mason jar with a glass cover and iron flip lock. He pried the corroded bar down and opened the jar where Peter kept his key. Using the rusty key, Connor jiggled it carefully into the lock. With a groan from the aging hinges the door swung open and he was in.

Once inside, he left the door open to air out the cabin. He lit a propane lamp that hung from the ceiling and another on a small card table that sat in the middle of the room. Looking around, he felt like he had stepped back in time, surrounded by the warm memories of his childhood. The side of the camp that faced the forest down to the river had a window which let in all the light the trees would allow. Two windows on either side of the door where Connor had entered attempted the same feat. On the countertop sat Grandpa's old thermos, a can of instant coffee, and two bottles of propane for the lamps. Connor knew there was a tank underneath the counter that connected to the two-burner stove and, through the wall of the camp, the grill. A dusty, two-sided sink protruded into the countertop. There was also a water hook up that no one had been out to mess with yet that year. Along the wall above the sink, nails jutted out from two-by-fours on which hung an old cast-iron frying pan, a pot, two spatulas, and Papa Peter's filet knife. Under the counter were a few drawers full of silverware and random odds and ends. Two bunk beds sat in the back of the camp, screwed together at the hands of his grandfather, just like everything else inside. Connor stood for a minute and marveled at the pitched roof and the exposed rafters with old fishing rods and paddles laid across them. The wooden floor was dusty, and the walls let in a faint draft and sliver of light. The windows seemed to each have a discernable layer of grime and at least a small spiderweb in each corner, much like the entrance. He thought of the hard work his grandfather and father had put into the place when they built it all those years ago. He wasn't even alive when the camp was initially built, but it grew to serve all of them as a sanctuary and place of bonding for years. Connor finally realized how special it was. He imagined a time before he was born: his father carrying two-by-fours and buckets of screws and nails down the freshly cut path and Peter providing as much instruction as Walt could handle, the way fathers always do.

Settling in, Connor put his food into a cooler that slid out from under one of the bunks. This would serve him much better than the soft cooler he had brought. Under the other bunks there were totes containing flashlights, batteries, extra propane bottles, bungee cords, loads of tackle, toilet paper, and pretty much any other essential that could have been imagined over the thirty-year life of the place.

Walking behind the camp Connor lifted a piece of plywood that was attached with a hinge to the side of the camp. The plywood angled down from the camp about six feet out and created a makeshift storage area. Connecting two hook-and-eye latch locks and a couple of two-by-fours sticking off the side of the camp, Connor opened it up. He had been around for this creation and remembered his grandfather's pride when Walter thought of it to protect the canoe at the camp instead of dragging it with them through the woods each time they came. Underneath the canoe was a weedwhacker and a gas can. Connor immediately went to work. Even if no one else was going to come up this summer, it felt right for Papa Peter's camp to be well maintained. The inside was always dusty, it was a camp after all, but they kept it picked up inside and orderly outside. He removed fallen branches, cleaned up the long grass and small shrubs, and lastly dispatched the spiderwebs. In a half hours' time Connor felt good about himself. He had started to sweat a little, something he never did back at his job in the city unless it was from the stress of a deadline. This was different, this was hard work. It was labor for an end result. He felt satisfied.

Taking a gulp of his water Connor sat down in the neatly trimmed clearing outside the camp on a freshly wiped folding chair. He had lugged his rod and gear out to the yard and was ready to tie on his tackle and head down to the river. His excitement grew as he opened the box. He hadn't been up to the camp in a couple years and his tackle box was covered in dirt and filth from sitting on the floor of his parents' garage. Here he had everything for all sorts of fishing: flies for a fly rod he didn't have with him, big spoons for trolling rods on the lake, bobbers from when he would take his sisters to the local ponds and teach them how to reel in little perch. He had tackle ranging from Mooselooks and Rooster Tails all the way down to spinnerbaits and rubber worms. A lot of different fishing could be done with the tackle accumulated over the years but what he was really after was his brook trout gear.

Connor grabbed his fishing rod, with the Zebco 33 reel attached. He knew it wasn't a top market item, but it had never failed him. He checked his monofilament line which seemed to still be in good shape. He considered changing it out but was too eager to get to the river. Reaching into the tackle box he grabbed a swivel and began looping the fishing line through the eye of the swivel, then around the line itself, then back down the hole he had created, and pulled it to make a tight knot. Connor clipped the tiny excess line with his pocket knife, which was now attached to his hip. He dug back into his box for a package of Snell's number six hooks with trout spinners and attached one via the swivel clip. Knowing how quick the water can get in that part of the brook he also grabbed a tin split shot, avoiding the now illegal lead split shot in his tackle box. He found a spot about eighteen inches up the line and secured the split shot on it with his teeth. It was an act that his father taught him and that made his mother cringe when she saw him rigging up in the garage. She was always thinking about how much his braces cost when he was twelve and how smart it was to be biting a piece of metal.

Check your riggin' before we get down to the water, don't wanna have to tie on a new set while your father and I catch all the fish! Peter Hennessey's words of wisdom rang true and Connor checked his—it was tight as a drum.

From his tackle box Connor brought his hooks with spinners, swivels, and split shots, stuffing them into his breast pocket before buttoning it. He popped open the cooler and grabbed one of the cartons of crawlers. They were still nice and cold, and he placed them into his soft cooler with a bottle of water he had filled in the camp. He strapped the cooler across his chest as he had on the way in, then spun it to his back so he would have room to cast. With his rod in hand and light gear packed up, Connor closed and locked the camp door behind him and shoved the old, rusted key into his buttoned breast pocket. Then he headed for the river.

Chapter 7

Side stepping down the bank in a pair of old water-proof boots he had left at the camp years prior, Connor neared the river. The old boots were a little snug, which was good because the steep bank was damp and the earth beneath his feet began to slide. He carefully maneuvered his way close to the water and stepped out onto a flat clear spot where the stream bent slightly around a corner. Setting his gear down and wrapping a half of a crawler onto the barbed hook he tossed out his first cast and watched the river take his spinner and all the attached tackle down with the current. The trout spinner rolled over and over providing just the flash he had hoped would get some attention. He reeled up slowly and kept his eyes angled toward the bending river. He wanted to get his bait into the deep cold water but not so deep that it would get hung up on bottom or curled around the bank. There was always a technical element to fishing these tight corners with moving water and he loved it. Cast after cast he worked his way carefully down river along the damp bank, coming closer to the water when possible and moving away as the bank steepened or trees blocked his cast. The blackflies were the only thing getting a bite but Connor didn't mind as he swatted them away with his hat and reapplied his Ben's. It was all worth it if he could feel the strike of a brook trout.

Connor had no luck as he moved down river for the better part of an hour. Then, he broke a corner and saw a Godsend, a beaver dam. The trees dragged across the river had dammed up the water to a degree. The water was a little high and moved quickly with the recent heavy rain and it flowed over the top of the dam. With his rubber waterproofs, Connor stepped carefully out onto the dam. He knew that finding his footing was crucial if he wanted to stay dry and not be shot down the cold river. He wiggled his feet into two spots that felt solid but that he could step out of if he were to lose his balance. This was an old trick his father taught him after he watched a family friend sprain his ankle and ultimately still fall into the river.

As cold water rushed over his feet, he casted in front of the beaver dam where the water appeared deep and pooling and was met with a quick strike. With a stiffening of his wrists and a twist of his shoulders he set the hook and the fish began to fight. He reeled up, keeping the line taut, and without yanking or pulling he brought him in.

Don't horse him! Keep that line tight, his grandfather's words again coming into his head. Now he had to maneuver the fish over to him on the beaver dam without getting the line tangled in the downed trees and debris. Connor worked the fish to the surface and brought his pole to his hip, then he grabbed the tip of the pole with one hand and the line with the other. It was important once the trout was out of the water to get him in hand quickly so he wouldn't wriggle off. He didn't have the luxury of the net that was in the canoe, so he swung the line with the fish above the debris in the river and into his hand. This was a beautiful native Maine brook trout. Dark near the top of his back and lighter moving down to the belly. It had spot markings, a square tail, classic wave-like lines on the back, and a touch of white on the leading edge of the fins. This trout was about eight inches long but well-fed. It was a keeper. The fish wiggled briefly as Connor slid his hand down its back, held him tightly without squeezing, and removed the hook. He then placed his thumb through the gill of the fish and pressed toward his index finger at the back. Using his other hand for support, he applied pressure breaking the spine and giving the fish a quick death. The trout stopped moving and, satisfied beyond recent memory, Connor popped the fish into the cooler and tied on another crawler.

Briefly, the beaver dam was a honey hole and Connor nabbed three more keepers. They were all seven or eight-inch brook trout, the type that are delicious to eat, which he fully intended to do. Standing on the dam, Connor looked out down the river. A twig in the stream twisted down in clockwise circles, showing the speed of the current. The wind had picked up and blew softly back in his face. It had gotten slightly cooler with the breeze, but it was a great trade off to be free of the blackflies. The mosquitos and blackflies could be relentless during that time of year. Both were thick, and the blackflies were constantly swarming, getting into ears, eyes, nose and even throat if you opened your mouth at the wrong time. Reapplication of Ben's and praying for a breeze was key. Examining his sunglasses on top of his hat he noticed that the DEET had eaten off the outer layer of sealant on the plastic, but it was either toxic bug repellent or inexorable insects. Fortunately, the breeze brought in air that was refreshing and piney. The shrubs and long grass on the river bank began to quiver and shudder in the wind. In some ways it was incredibly peaceful and in others almost eerie. The wind made Connor realize how alone he was standing in the middle of the river, with his closest companion a moose a few miles upstream and whatever else lay out of sight. A few ominous clouds moved in front of the afternoon sun and the temperature seemed to instantly drop a couple degrees further.

Without a bite in his last fifteen casts, and after trying the quick water on the other side of the beaver dam, Connor made his way cautiously off and back to the bank. He would try for another half hour working downstream then would trek back to camp in a quarter of the time. He worked his way along the edge of the river. The bank had flattened a bit and swale grass cropped up, jutting out over where the riverbank turned to dry land. Connor was careful, avoiding hazards with every step as what looked like a meadow often behaved like a marsh. He looked to the tree line and surveyed the spruce and fir before setting his eyes onto a large eastern pine standing above everything else near it. There were two saplings not far off from it in the distance. Around one bend and then another he continued, casting, reeling, and walking.

One more bend, he said to himself. Walking quietly in the tall grass and having reeled up already, Connor moved around an overgrown shrub that had obstructed his view of the next leg of the brook. At that moment he felt a wind gust blow back upstream into his face. He closed his eyes and let the fresh air wash over him.

Standing on the river bank motionless and silent, his head finally cleared and his spirit was high. Connor opened his eyes and broke the small line of undergrowth among the wavering grass. His heart again began to pound. There was movement on the horizon.

Chapter 8

About a hundred yards away a black mass bobbed in the tall grass and then stepped to the edge of the river. Two smaller black figures then tumbled toward the larger one. It was a black bear with her two cubs. Connor clung to a tree nearby and watched them, completely frozen. Black bears are not typically dangerous or violent, but they can be if startled or protecting their young. It was rare to see a black bear as they often smell humans long before humans see them. He had caught glimpses of them a few times before as they bounded off. Stories of bear encounters entered his mind. A few years earlier a close friend had jumped one when tracking a buck during hunting season. It happened in the woods of northern Maine in November and the bear charged him. His friend, a seasoned hunter, rapidly fired three rounds from his .30/06 rifle into the bear before it was finally stopped and ended up just ten feet away. Connor had only a jackknife; no match for that beautiful beast. With that image in his mind he slid back among the small trees and shrubbery. The sound and direction of the wind must have allowed him to fish undetected. He moved back up stream quickly, occasionally glancing back. As his heart rate began to normalize he thought about Peter. He remembered his grandfather telling him the importance of paying attention to his surroundings and respecting the animals of the Northwoods. *How'd you like it if some Tom, Dick, or Harry came stomping into your living room? Not very much eh? I didn't think so.* Every lesson handed down by Peter Hennessey had a personalized spin on it and if you weren't laughing when he was done talking then you probably weren't listening.

Connor made his way back to camp, moving steadily with the wind now at his back. There were no black-flies or mosquitos to fend off anymore with the wind, but he figured it best not to encounter that bear with a bag full of trout. Dropping his gear and pole off against the side of the cabin, he brought the cooler with the fish down to the river. A flat stump made for a nice cutting board and Connor laid all four fish out next to each other. Taking the first, he held the body against the stump and ran his knife up under the fin closest to the head of the fish. He then twisted the sharp blade perpendicularly and made a smooth cut through the bones, removing the head. Connor turned the fish in his hand, positioning the dorsal fin against his palm so the headless trout lay belly up. He slit open the gut just above the tail and ran the knife straight to the head of the fish. With the nail of his thumb he entered the body of the fish and pushed in toward the spine. Following the knife slit with his thumb, he removed the guts and emptied them into the river, using the cold, clear river water as a rinse.

Chummin' the waters, boys, as Papa Peter always used to say. He, like most New England natives, held a special place in his heart for the movie *Jaws*. After but-

44

terflying the remainder of the trout in a similar fashion and rinsing his hands in the river he brought them back up to the cabin.

Relighting the propane lamps and hooking up the gas to the two-burner stove, Connor started preparing his fish fry. He took the cast iron skillet off the nail on the wall and let it warm on the burner. Tossing a dollop of butter into the pan, he worked it around as it sizzled and coated the inside. He found some breadcrumbs under the counter. They had to be at least a year old, but he knew they'd work. No eggs on this trip so the egg wash was out, but butter and breadcrumbs would work as a solid pair. With the cast iron hot, he threw the semi-breaded fish into the pan with another unhealthy amount of butter and they began to brown on the outside. The smell evoked nostalgia of weekends there as a kid when his grandfather would cook up a slew of fish while his father built a roaring fire outside in the fire pit. With the spatula Connor scooped up the last of the fish, each one looking golden brown on the outside, perfectly cooked just like he was taught. He set the fish on the card table and quickly spun together a Canadian Club and Canada Dry mixer, fifty-fifty. Sitting down he pulled at the spine of the fish and it came out with most of the small bones intact. Taking two bites, he was in heaven. It tasted just as he remembered. His satisfaction grew along with his sense of freedom and contentedness.

Nothing is better than earning your dinner, he said to himself. Washing it down with a gulp of whiskey and ginger ale, he went outside to use the last of the daylight to get a fire going.

Dragging in dead but dry birch along with twigs and

bark, Connor made a stack next to the fire pit and went to the plywood storage spot to grab a few sticks of cedar. Holding a piece of cedar with his left hand and guiding the blade of the hatchet into the top, he tapped the two on a flat rock by the pit. The cedar split enough that he could remove his left hand and proceeded to tap the half-split cedar up and then down to split it entirely. After splitting up a dozen or so sticks of kindling, Connor crumpled up an old copy of the local newspaper from his hometown. *The Rolling Thunder Express* must have been five years old, but it was dry, and its age made no difference to the fire. Lighting the pile of paper underneath the teepee of kindling with some matches he found in the camp, the split cedar quickly caught. Connor fed the blaze from his heap of branches, sticks, twigs, and bark, and the evening breeze fanned the flames to create a nice glow.

Chapter 9

It was dusk now. The wind stayed mild but steady. The trees swayed and the sun had just set. The temperature dropped off quickly and Connor grabbed a sweater from one of the totes. It was a 1996 Patriots AFC Championship hoody with more than a few holes burnt into it from past campfires, but it served its purpose. He then grabbed his old, half-melted, AM/FM turn dial radio from under one of the bunks. A previous trip had included a few extra whiskey drinks and the radio had paid the price, being left too close to the fire. He walked back out to the yard with a bite of fish in hand.

Just then he heard the snap of a twig, quickly followed by a second. There was movement near the trail where he had entered earlier that day. He reached for his flashlight but it was no longer on his belt. He could feel his heart pounding in his chest again. He thought there was no way that a bear would be so brazen, but anything is possible. The sound kept coming. It was a little way off and seemed to be getting closer. His mouth dried as he tried to swallow the last bites of the fish he was chewing. He grabbed the knife off his hip and peered through the smoke from the fire. It was crackling now and provided some light toward the path.

Connor snapped the blade open and stood hunched, staring over the flames toward the trail. He wasn't sure what was out there, if anything, but it certainly sounded like something big moving toward him through the thick overgrown footpath. *Coyotes maybe*, he thought, but it didn't seem likely. He moved around the fire slowly, his eyes level with the wood line.

Suddenly, a voice boomed, "Is that any way to greet your father?" It was Walt. "Put that knife away boy, before you hurt yourself."

His heart rate settled back into range. He snapped the blade of his knife closed and slid it back onto his belt. As Walt got closer to the fire his large shadow became a silhouette and eventually Connor could see his face. His figure and gait were strikingly similar to Connor's, but his age showed in his face and eyes as they flashed against the light of the flames.

"Hope you saved some of *my* whiskey for me," Walt said, approaching the fire. Connor couldn't tell if he was angry that he had swiped it from the house or happy that his son had trekked it in for what would now be for the both of them.

"Plenty of CC and ginger on the table. Trout right there too. Help yourself," Connor replied with an air of quiet confidence. He had done well setting up camp and was feeling pretty good about it.

"Looking like a good fire kid, you got enough wood on there?" Walt asked rhetorically. It was a modest blaze which apparently was not up to snuff.

"Grab a drink and something to eat. I'll tend the fire." Connor diverted his father. At this point in their lives this was the most convivial greeting either could have hoped for.

Snapping a few large branches in half from a fallen tree, Connor dragged them over and threw them onto the orange flame. A nice bed of coals was just starting to coat the bottom of the pit. The branches popped and hissed, and Connor hoped that his father wouldn't come out until that sound of wet wood had passed.

Walt eventually lumbered out with a drink, which was likely not his first of the day, and sat down with a mouthful of trout. He wore blue jeans and a red flannel shirt, both of which were very worn. His shirt was half unbuttoned revealing a faded t-shirt underneath that was frayed at the collar. His salt and pepper hair was hidden under the baseball hat he wore at all times unless he was working. The fire illuminated his five o'clock shadow and as he peered into the blaze Connor could make out the slight wrinkles in the corners of both eyes.

"Good work, kid. No eggs, but good work." Walt couldn't help but find the fault in things, even when he was grateful and enjoyed them. "Where'd you catch these, up river or down river? How many did you end up with today?" His father continued, as if they had just spoken the day prior, although it felt much different for them both. His level of comfort alone showed the current drink likely wasn't his second of the day either.

"Worked my way down the river, stayed on this side, found a bit of a honey hole with a beaver dam probably a half mile down. Water pooled up pretty good, nice deep spot," Connor responded. "I didn't know you were coming up. Surprised to see you. Didn't look like anyone had been up here yet this year," he said gently, prodding his father.

"This is my first trip up. I have been working a lot

but more locally. Less travel, just an overnight here and there," Walt replied in between bites.

"Everything all right at the house? Saw Mom, she seemed well." Connor continued his best attempt at small talk.

"Oh yea, all is well," Walt replied, running out of fish to occupy the gaps in conversation. He rubbed his hands together and then wiped them on his pants to free himself from any fish remnants and because anything was more comfortable than being still.

"Well, good. I'm glad to hear it," Connor finished with this pleasantry and stared into the fire.

Remembering the radio, he reached down and flipped the switch to the "on" position. He turned the knob through the static while bending the antenna this way and that until something started to come through.

Sixty-sixty degrees here on a beautiful night for base-ball at Fenway Park. Heading into the top half of the fifth inning after the Red Sox scored three times in the bottom of the fourth on a two-run double by Xander Bogarts and an RBI single by Dustin Pedroia to put Boston on top four to two. Rodriguez set to take the mound, he's been sharp so far but faces the meat of this Toronto order here in the fifth...

"Hitting many games this year?" Walt asked, breaking into the broadcast.

"I've been to one so far. By the time I get home from work a lot of nights it's already the second or third inning," Connor responded trailing off. The effort for civility was apparent. He didn't want to change the topic, just listen to the game and watch the fire.

"I've been waiting for you," his father said, looking down. Moving the conversation away from baseball wasn't comfortable for either of them.

"I got a letter, I know you got one too. When your mother told me you surfaced at the house I knew what for," Walt paused. There was more to explain but at the same time there wasn't. This was Peter Hennessey conking their heads together from the grave.

"I should have been at the wake. It took me getting this letter to realize that. I have been buried at work," Connor offered, staring at his feet and fidgeting in his folding chair.

"Learned from the best. Doing what you are supposed to do, working hard," his father replied without looking up, unable to connect.

Connor waited for Walt to speak again but he didn't. He just sat there quietly staring off into the fire. His guilt for not being at his grandfather's service returned, it made him a little sick to his stomach. He began to wonder at his father's true thoughts, so often a mystery to him. Connor thought about asking why he believed they were both up there, or why he hadn't called. Then, he thought better of it; let good enough lie.

The rest of the night by the fire was quiet but not awkward. They sat there and listened to the game and began to feel a little more at peace with each other, however fragile that feeling was. After a few drinks and a radio pause for station identification, Connor retold a story that included all three of them. They were out trolling for togue and brookies on Moosehead Lake back when he was still a teenager. Connor and a buddy had waited for Walt and Peter to hit the hay before raiding Grandpa Peter's cooler. Peter and Walt had known all along but let them get away with it anyway. Walt followed by sharing another story and reminiscing about

Peter and his childhood, something that Connor had rarely seen him do.

Peter had been in the Marines and fought in Korea. He was a big, strong, powerful man in his youth. As is the case with many young men, he did not have the patience and foresight he would hold later in life. He came back from the war harder than he was when he went over. It took him some time to settle into being Papa Peter, the beloved patriarch that Connor and his siblings would know and love.

After the war he met his beloved DeDe and they quickly started a family. Walter was born a few years after his brother Paul. They grew up in a modest home on the outskirts of town where his father taught them the value of a day's labor from a young age. Peter believed in the American Dream. He believed in good, honest, work and he instilled that value every day. That is how his father taught him and that was what he would impart unto his boys. They worked on farms shoveling cow shit, pulling chickens in the chicken houses, haying, and anything else that would help make money. Peter had the boys ride their bikes from the country into town for different odd jobs he would line up for them. Some of the wages contributed to the family, but Peter let them keep most for themselves. For him it was as much to instill the value of hard work as anything else.

Peter was tough on the boys but loved them both dearly. When they behaved they got to go fishing with the men and hear stories from the olden days. When they weren't so good, Peter had no problem using the belt. As Walt got a little older he got the belt or a slap upside the head a little more often until he straightened around. Peter always wanted what was best for his family. Even though in his youth he had a short fuse, most of the time he was in the right and the boys needed discipline. After all, he was a military man. He did his best to keep them on track; to mold honorable young men of the time that the family could be proud of.

Despite having no formal education beyond high school, Peter was bright. After the war he needed to find work right away as DeDe was with child almost immediately, so he took a position at the tannery. It was physically demanding, but it was a job. Besides, he enjoyed punching the clock and getting home to his adoring wife. As his sons grew up, he needed a steady paycheck and continued to work in that laborious position to maintain support rather than take any risks. Peter would always say to Paul and Walt: "Work hard so you don't have to do what I do." He always wanted them to excel in the classroom and pushed them to learn what it meant to work hard so that they could do something smart. And with what limited free time there was, he loved to have the boys out on the water. He was careful with the little money they had and over time was able to retire in what most people would consider the middle class.

And the 3–2 pitch, swung on and missed, he fooled Gonzalez on a breaking ball in the dirt for the third out of the inning. The bullpen able to get out of a jam and Toronto strands two at second and third. After seven and a half it's the Red Sox six and the Blue Jays four, Joe Castiglione's voice broke through the crackle of the fire and the static roar of the crowd on the radio.

Letting the fire burn out, the night became cold and

black. The wind could be heard through the trees along with the gentle, constant motion of the river down below. They hadn't talked too much of a game plan, but Connor knew his father would be up with first light ready to get out on the river; it was the thing they had most in common. A night that started with holding onto the quiet contention of the past wound down with the game and the flames. A small victory was won by both sides, a sort of conditional peace treaty for the greater good. Both remembered the escalation and tipping point a few years prior. But rather than dwell they both finished their drinks and let their heavy heads lead them into the cabin to get some rest.

Chapter 10

A culmination of events had been brewing for a long time. Most of the conflict between Walt and Connor went back almost ten years prior. The family had fallen on hard times and that landed squarely on Walt's shoulders. He was a sedulous worker and a self-made man. He had taken Peter's message to heart. He worked at least twenty-five hours a week all through high school and college, eventually able get his college degree in business and pay for it himself. After years of employment in sales, supporting his growing family, and jumping from company to company, he got his big idea. While working on the lawnmower one night in the garage, he realized he had to drive twenty miles after a full day's work to get a missing tool. At that moment, he figured out what he wanted to do. He was going to open a hardware store on his own and become a local small business owner. This was a project that could bring him pride and the potential for growth.

Walt opened Hennessy's Toolbox in 1999. Anita ran the register while the kids played around the store with the family dog Eddie, knocking over wheel barrels and horsing around with each other. It was a good time for the family, but like many things in life it was stressful for Walt and he was always focused on work. He put everything he had into the store and loved it. The satisfaction was his reward for the labor pains. If there was something to know about a product he knew it, if there was something people in town needed he had it, and if there was a way he could make more money without jeopardizing quality, he found it. He grew the business for eight years, expanding and carrying more products to suit the community needs. Everyone in town knew Walt at Hennessey's Toolbox.

Most mornings Peter would be in the store lending his thoughts on business while drinking the free coffee and telling stories with other vets and townspeople. In the summer Connor would work for his father stocking shelves, doing inventory, and running the register. It was sunny times for father and son. Between working at the store together, Walt coaching Connor's baseball team, and going fishing on the weekend the two were inseparable.

Then came the crash in '08. People stopped spending money as everyone scaled back and came for the essentials only. Walt hung on, trying to figure out how to keep the business afloat. He put in seventy hours a week, did the jobs of three men to cover costs, but in the end it wasn't enough. By 2010, he filed for bankruptcy and ended up out of business; he had failed. The business he proudly built and hoped his son would one day own crumbled before him.

It had been three rough years. After the initial downturn and through to the collapse it consumed Walt and at some point, ate him up. He was no longer able to coach baseball. He never got out to fish with his son or father. Walt began to take out his frustration on his family, often becoming irritated and even more often than that, drunk. Time he once spent at the hardware store or at his kids' baseball and softball games he now spent at the Elks Lodge. Walt began coming home late, much of the time stewed on whiskey. He found the outlet to his frustration in pushing Connor. On some level Walt felt he had failed himself and his family and he wouldn't let that happen to his boy. Connor, however, was doing all right. He had lost some focus as teenagers tend to once they discover girls, and a few times he had been "fresh," as his mother called it, which meant some punishment, but overall, he was a regular kid. In his youth a little redirection from Walt was common, but more and more frequently Walt began to rant aimlessly about how Connor wasn't doing enough. It was never enough, not in school or hours spent at part time jobs. It always needed to be more. Walt thought he was doing the right thing: it was stern parenting. However, Connor felt he was always locked in a battle with the man who had been his longest standing ally. The disputes pinned the two against each other more and more. Connor became angrier and more distant. He soon slipped into an adolescence of selfishness and disrespect. When the two did talk Connor filled the conversation with quick-witted remarks to rebut his father's verbal onslaughts. These skirmishes continued to a point where it seemed less important to say the right thing and more important to give the last word before one party stormed off. The strained relationship continued into college. On winter break Walt berated Connor in front of his friends about how he lacked focus and discipline because he hadn't officially committed to a major after his first semester. That struck Connor hard and he fired back, "I can see where all your hard work got you."

He had been the scapegoat in this maddening breakdown for too long, but as soon as he said it he wished he hadn't. Connor had kicked a man when he was down. However frustrating, he knew it was still his father, who in his own misguided way wanted the best for his only son. After the incident they both buried their heads in the proverbial sand and didn't speak for four months.

Connor became more self-involved and his thoughts became largely limited to staying out of town, away from his father, and away from his home. At times, he would freeze out his sisters and mother, and visits to his grandparents became less frequent. He had been a good, well-intentioned boy but was no longer like that smiling kid at the hardware store.

Although their interactions became less frequent over the next few years, both would become more and more withdrawn so despite no direct conflict, family gatherings had the feeling of a Cold War summit.

One weekend after finishing college Connor came home for a visit. He had been busy interviewing at different competitive companies, much like the one he now worked for. The grind of hurry up and wait had gotten to him and he wanted to relax and see some childhood friends. Thus far Connor had avoided Walt and thought that for this trip it was still the best approach. It was a Saturday night and he had gone out with a few old high school buddies to blow off some steam. He came up the driveway to his father waiting for him in the garage with a bottle of Jim Beam, half gone, and an earful locked and loaded. His father, still a bull of a man and a young looking fifty-five years old, was pacing back and forth.

"Came home to have some drinks did ya? I help you get through college and you come home to drink my beer and screw around with your idiot friends? You gonna get to work at some point or just waste your whole life?" Walt questioned. He was riled up, drunk and pouring sweat. His sleeves were rolled up exposing his forearms and his bulging veins teemed with bourbon. His eyes were wild and blood shot red. He looked at Connor strangely, almost like he didn't recognize his own son. He glared angrily and without compassion. The alcohol had forced that from him by now.

"I am working on it. I have things lined up for next week, just wanted to pay a visit to these guys. My idiot friends are doing well, by the way." Connor repelled the initial verbal lumps, but his demeanor seemed to only irritate Walt further. He had taken help from his father to go to college and as their relationship soured over the years he made less of an effort to show his appreciation. This was something that bothered each of them from their respective positions. Connor didn't want the help but needed it and Walt wanted to help but also demanded the respect for his sacrifice. Connor had been working diligently to land the job he wanted all while working the same student job that helped get him through college. As usual, it wasn't good enough. Tensions ran high and Walt continued to rant.

"Have things lined up do ya? What exactly do you have lined up?" Walt condescendingly asked. His line of questions functioned rhetorically because he was not able to hear any responses. The booze had deafened him to reason. He was enraged. He continued to pace.

Connor looked at him sideways, frustrated. He

shook his head. They had been down this road a few times and it never went very well. There had been yelling in the past and he hoped to avoid that this time, so he passively deflected and started to walk away. Walt took this as dismissive and disrespectful.

"Don't you walk away from me when I am talking to you!" Walt growled.

He grabbed Connor, squeezing his shoulders, bringing his red face only a few inches from Connor's.

A milli-second passed and Connor shook loose, this time not with frustration or fear but rage. Connor was a man now, as big as he was likely going to be, shorter than his father but stocky and strong. The war of words was over. He shoved his father off and knocked him back a few feet. Walt came roaring back. A boiling point had been reached after a long simmer. The two were tangled in locked arms, slamming into three sides of the garage, knocking over rakes, shovels, and anything else hanging on the unfinished walls. The garage seemed to explode with the sound of two bodies destroying everything not bolted down. They knocked over the work bench, spilling tools and a bucket of screws all over the floor. Walt took the first swing with a glancing blow that landed behind Connor's ear. In recovery, Connor unloaded a right hook that snapped his father's head back, making enough contact with his chin to open it up. The two locked up again and Walt's strength showed as he threw his son to the ground like a rag doll. Connor hit his head on the way down cutting a chunk of hair and skin from the back of his skull. It would scar eventually and leave a tiny bald spot. In that moment Connor wasted no time and leapt back to his feet, the two of them mere inches apart. This was all it took, the detachment from a violent engagement and they both knew it was over. Walt scoffed at him with seething wrath. Blood dripped from his chin and more ran down his arm from scraping against a nail on the wall. He stormed off and slammed the side door to the garage causing a canoe paddle to fall from the rafters. Connor sat down in disbelief at what had happened. Both of them finally snapped and Connor's emotions ran the gamut. He was angry, embarrassed, and unsure of what to do next. He sat in the garage shaking his head and looking at his trembling hands.

This event cost the two of them a relationship they once cherished. Connor felt he lost a father, a baseball coach, and a fishing buddy. For Walt, it was his only son that he loved and tried to mold in his own troubled way. Unfortunately, the family trait of thick-headedness didn't skip any generations. Instead of learning from the scuffle they both put their heads down like stubborn old mules and pushed forward separately.

Over time the feeling of resentment grew and it became the norm to avoid contact. Walt had bounced from job to job after losing the business but realized it was time to snap out of it, to pull himself up by the bootstraps like his father would have done. He took up a steady job as a business consultant. After all, he had managed to be a success prior to the crash. The few years of floundering were over. Connor knew through the family grapevine that Walt was back to his old self. And Walt knew, however peripherally, that Connor was successful and established in the city. Both felt bitterness but mostly shame. It was easier to bury that feeling and go to work than deal with it.

The melee in the garage was four years before

Peter's death. Even with effort from the family to ease tensions both Connor and Walt found a way to be busy with anything but reconciliation. Towards the end it was all Peter would talk about.

Chapter 11

Waking the next morning in his sleeping bag Connor felt the cold draft of fresh air coming in from around the aging windows. It was light out, but the sun had not yet been able to impact the temperature. Even though it was the beginning of June, temperatures were often in the forties or low fifties this early in the mornings. Walt was already up and moving about. Anything and everything could be heard in the wooden insulation-free structure. The cool-to-the-touch floorboards creaked as Connor made his way to the common area. He could see Walt had gotten into their favorite morning meal when Downeast on the river: Mrs. Dunster's donuts and coffee. Connor downed a half liter of water before starting his breakfast. He felt a little foggy but was determined to power through it. He never wanted to show weakness to his father and without the help of whiskey, his guard was back up.

"About time you are up. How you feeling kid?" his father asked, never passing on a chance to let Connor know he was awake before him, as if age and insomnia were things of merit.

"Never better. Let's finish these up and get on the water," Connor started in with a chipper response.

"I'll finish up here and then we can drag that square

stern down to the water. I'll make a second trip up for the motor and gas can," Walt said, walking out the front door and unfolding his chair on the lawn in the sun. He sat down and squinted through aging eyes trying to maneuver his large fingers to tie a swivel onto his line.

"Throw it all in the canoe, we can manage. If you don't think we can I'll throw that motor over my shoulder and lug it down," Connor replied, eager to get moving and demonstrate his worth.

"All right bub, we'll put it in and lug it together." Without looking up Walt could sense he wasn't dragging a boy out of bed to go fishing anymore.

The early morning of tense civility gave way to more natural conversation as the two of them felt each other out, just as they had done the night before. Neither was fully comfortable but somewhere inside they both wanted to get along like the old days.

Walt snapped the motor onto the board at the stern and tightened the bolts to fasten the 5-horse Yamaha motor on securely. Sliding the square stern of the canoe into the river Walt stepped into the center and smoothly slid back to his seat at the rear. Holding the rope, Connor maneuvered into the bow. He then threw the rope behind him into the canoe. With the propeller out of the water, they pushed off and began to float for a moment, slowly down river.

They were back in the positions they had assumed so many times before. His father always drove, and Connor helped to navigate the banks and spot beaver dams and debris in the quick, clear water. Walt dropped the propeller, primed the motor, and pulled the cord. On the third yank it fired up. After a quick choke, he twisted the vibrating throttle handle and they began their way up river in silence. The sound of the canoe moving against the current and creating a tiny wake gave them both some time to enjoy the cool, tranquil morning. Talking was not necessary and even a little difficult which, at this moment, was perfect. Traveling up river both father and son were satisfied and excited to wet lines. The early sun beamed off the ripples in the water creating a shimmer that reflected the ambient morning. Twisting and bending in an S-shaped fashion they traversed up the tight windy river. The pair felt restored with the smell of crisp morning air and the breeze in their faces.

After a few miles Walt cut the motor and let them drift into an eddy where the river gets fat and the churning pools trapped by steeper banks allow the canoe to spin slowly in place. The spinning water made little whirlpools appear from nowhere and disappear just as quickly. Approaching the bank Connor tied off to an overhanging birch tree that was half dead from a storm but didn't appear to be going anywhere.

"Hey kid, you gonna hog that thermos all day or can the old man have some coffee?" This was Walt's subtle way of asking for something. In previous years Connor may have snapped a quick-witted reply back just to prod his father, but Walt shot him a rare smile, so he gently tossed the thermos over.

"All yours, old man," Connor said. Both of them used to call his grandfather that, and they both acknowledged the fact without saying a word.

Unhooking the size-six barbed hook from the third eye of his ultra-light rod, Connor ripped a nightcrawler in half and put it on, doubling it over as the crawler was long even after being halved. He threw the other half to his father. "Don't say I never did anything for ya."

Now both ready to get a line in the water, they quickly went to work. Sitting in silence, casting and reeling, they were fishing together for the first time in years. They hadn't even sat in the same room together in quite some time, and now they were sitting in the same canoe as they had so many times before.

"No action up here bub, they got tails. Let's see if we can find 'em. Untie us would ya?" Walt instructed.

They floated down river without using the motor, spinning backward then forward and letting the current take them downstream. Casting and reeling, casting and reeling. Then, following a tributary that would come back into the main river, they hit a beaver dam and their eyes lit up. They got the paddles out and angled toward the bank, beaching the bow of the canoe on the dam near the bank and crawling out through the front. The beavers had used some of the nearby alders in damming the river and the markings from their teeth could be plainly seen. The wetlands were plentiful with these shrub-like trees along the riverbank. The Hennessey boys climbed aboard the dam in hopes it would prove to be a fishing haven.

"Nice deep pool here, this is the spot," Connor said. His father let him lead the way, something he never would have done years prior.

A first cast and Connor had an immediate strike. With the line taut, the ultra-light folded with the hit and Connor set the hook with a quick snap of his wrists. Reeling with the line tight the fish surfaced and tried to dive back down. Fighting the fish and trying to keep from tangling on the beaver dam Connor could hear his grandfather shouting, "Don't horse 'em, keep-'em tight, don't let 'em get hung up!" Then he realized it was not his beloved grandfather's voice but his own father's watching him from a few feet away. Connor felt like he was transported ten years back in time.

"Damn don't crank on 'em. Stay away from that downed tree, you'll never get 'em if he wraps your line under there." Peter had been an optimist and a teacher, his word taken at face value with encouragement. Walt on the other hand was always, if inadvertently, critical.

"I know what I am doing! Remember what you had for dinner last night?" Connor snapped, not looking away from the task at hand. Walt couldn't help himself. That's just what he did and how he was, even though he knew it drove his son crazy. Connor had what looked to be a beautiful, twelve-inch native brook trout, and as he grabbed the line the fish flopped and came off the hook. Normally, that may have been disappointing but with his father standing behind him Connor did all he could not to blow a gasket. For a moment he was back in the garage, looking fiercely over his shoulder, enraged.

Walt said nothing, the damage was done and again the tenuous relationship was frayed. Two men cut from the same cloth were at silent odds, rigid and frustrated. It was only ever partly about the fish, they both knew that. Although it was a hell of a nice fish, so really it was a compounded disappointment. Facing in opposite directions, their next handful of casts yielded nothing. What was a promising morning shifted quickly like the wind and they both got back into the canoe. Walt stepped over the net. This time the silent float down river was tense like so many past family dinners.

They set off again, intermittently casting and reeling in silence as they twisted and turned with the way of the canoe. Both were quietly hoping for the one thing that could return them to their jovial state: a strike. It was mid-morning now; the birds were chirping, and the sun warmed their shoulders. The same breeze from the day before began to pick up and the smell of pine wafted through the air. Wildflowers shimmied and a beaver jumped in the water right in front of the canoe, but still the two didn't speak. It was a quick revert to the way things had been. Stubborn to the core they had both forgotten why they were there and who brought them together as they internalized any and all feelings. If there had been a third party in the center of the canoe, he may have bailed into the cold water rather than deal with the icy conditions on the surface.

The canoe spun this way and that, and with the water higher than they would have wanted it, they moved faster downstream than anticipated.

*If I could keep my damn mouth shut...*Walt thought to himself.

*Why the hell do I let this stuff get to me? A bad day fishing is better than...*Connor simultaneously reflected, trying to embrace the Peter Hennessey credo, but the mood was all too familiar. It was easy to slip back into a bubbling feud. After all, he was his father's son. They passed the camp at a cruising speed, floating quickly in the current. Neither of these old mules were willing to give an inch and concede that maybe they should regroup. Unable to show weakness or defeat, they moved on down the river casting and reeling with no offers. The wind picked up blowing upstream right at them.

As the float continued and the river intensified, the current got stronger. Connor reeled up and thought about just letting the old man have it. It was beautiful out there on the river and they couldn't just get on the same team. *It was always the same*, he thought. He ran his hand over his head to settle down but instead his fingers found his bald spot. Connor's rage grew with the speed of the water and his father could see it.

As they broke a bend in the river the canoe bounced hard off a far bank and changed course for the other side of the narrow stretch of river. Neither of them grabbed a paddle or made any effort to slow down or tie off and they continued to barrel towards another bend. Connor was set to give him the business. Stuck in a canoe together he couldn't hold it in any longer. But just as he was about to speak they broke the corner and a very different reality set in.

All the rage in Connor's body vacated with the blood in his face as his heart leapt and pounded harder than it had ever before. The canoe was careening toward the bank around the bend in the river. The bow had bounced off the opposite bank again sending the stern blindly around the next corner. Walt was facing Connor and about to try to say something when he looked up to see his son's face ghostly white.

Chapter 12

Bear! A mother bear was on the bank with her two cubs, presumably the same one Connor had seen just a day ago. So much had happened he completely forgot about her. Now they were flying right at her with breakneck speed, and Walt, wheeling around, was about to meet her face to face. The natural inclination for both parties was to get the hell out of there but the canoe was out of control and within a few seconds it collided into the bank. The bear tried to leap back but with one front paw on the soft muddy river bank and the other in the river, she slipped. The rare misstep for this large but nimble creature made the bear agitated. Feeling threatened, she snorted and regained her balance for a moment as the stern slammed into the very bank she had almost fallen through. Walt, now seeing the danger, leaned forward. She bellowed and showed her teeth. She was a ball of muscle no less than two hundred and fifty pounds and larger than either man in the canoe. Her black fur sodden as mud and river water dripped from her massive paw. Instinctively, she took a swipe at Walt and for the first time in his life Connor saw fear in his father's eyes.

The bear tried again to push off and flee, but the bank was soggy from recent rain and high water and she nearly fell into the river, slipping worse the second time.

"Push off! Push off! Push off!" Walt shouted.

"We're stuck!" Connor hollered back. The propeller had blasted into the thick mud of the bank and was slow in coming out. An overgrown thicket scraped the side of the canoe holding it in the current as the river slowly tried to pull them downstream. The bear snorted again, angry and scared, protecting her cubs. Her brown muzzle showed her teeth as she let out a vicious, guttural sound. Her massive skull thrashed forward as she bucked upward and took another swipe at Walt. This time she tore part of his shirt with a quick and powerful slash. Both men began rocking and shaking to try and free themselves from the bank.

"Get us the hell outta here kid!" Walt hollered, with both hands on the sides of the craft shaking vigorously for his life. At that second Connor grabbed a paddle and slammed it through the thick shrub toward the bank, hitting a big branch or root. The bear raised up, seeming to gather herself before letting out a blood curdling growl that surely could have been heard all throughout the forest. Her lips snarled back, and her huge canine teeth showed. Just as she looked to give Walt, and possibly the whole canoe, a death blow Connor hit the thickest part of the shrub a second time and the vessel came free. The bear angrily watched them from the broken bank, snarling before bounding off into the woods a few seconds later with her cubs following closely behind. They had survived.

Chapter 13

"You're bleeding," Connor remarked. He looked concernedly at his father, forgetting any negative thoughts he ever had. "Are you all right?" Spinning backward again down the other side of the river Connor reached out and grabbed the bank to steady them to a halt.

Walt looked at Connor and began to laugh. "Damn! No one will ever believe that happened, you know?" He put his head in his hands and chuckled in disbelief. He was shaken up but almost in a state of shock.

"Dad, are you all right? Let's get out over here and I'll pull the canoe up. We need to have a look at you." Connor climbed out of the bow and pulled the canoe parallel with the bank of the river. He helped Walt out of the stern with one hand and held the rope with the other. Reaching down he grabbed the bow and pulled it up onto the shore into a grassy meadow leaving only the motor hanging over the river. The propeller, caked with mud and weeds, dripped dirty water into the swirling current.

"Let me see that," Connor examined. "She tore right through your shirt and hit the meat of your back."

"Nothing a little whiskey can't fix, right?" Walt replied, trying to brush it off, a classic old man technique.

"Alcohol wipes and bandages will do. She just clipped you but can't have that getting infected," Connor said, still in disbelief but functioning in an emergency just as he was raised to. "You are bleeding a bit back there so let me get that cleaned up and covered."

"Kid, hold on a sec. I'm all right." Walt grabbed Connor by the elbow.

"Dad, let me get this cleaned up. You won't have any story to tell if you get sick out here."

"You saved me. You saved both of us. I thought that she-bear was gonna tear me to shreds and flip the canoe for us both to be goners. I have never experienced anything like that in my whole life. Damn, I just can't believe it. You saved me. You saved us both." Walt welled up, his eyes red as he embraced Connor, squeezing him. Connor felt like a kid again, but in a good way this time.

"Damn it, all right. That's enough of that, kid. Slap some alcohol on this little cut and wrap it up. Let's get back to camp. We have things to do," Walt wiped his eyes quickly and exhaled sharply to regain his composure. This was the most emotion he had let escape since being in the funeral parlor alone with Peter for the last time.

They got back in the canoe, Connor helped his father ease in slowly to not make a mess of the clean bandages he had just applied from the first aid kit.

"Should already be clotting up back there. Try not to do anything to rip those gashes back open," Connor said, instructing his father with the compassion of his grandfather. Connor took over at the stern and after freeing the propeller of river mud, guided them up river back to camp.

Chapter 14

When they returned Connor helped Walt out of the canoe again and set his father down in a chair. Pulling the canoe up onto land, he dragged it to the storage spot and lugged the motor over to set it underneath. He split some kindling from the cedar they had left drying in the sun and crumpled a few pages of the *Rolling Thunder Express* to start another fire. He brought his father a blanket for his shoulders and a whiskey-ginger to help with the pain. Just a day prior much of this would have been inconceivable. Instead, Walt sat quietly by the fire watching his boy take care of everything. It was a refreshing spring afternoon and the day had cooled significantly. Walt was becoming sore. In and out of the canoe, sleeping on a bunk, and nearly getting mauled to death by a bear were good reasons to stay put in his chair. His pride swelled along with his wound as he watched Connor cook the remains of the cleaned trout that had been kept on ice overnight in a cooler under the bunk. He could smell the delicious pan fry and, perhaps more importantly, finally began to relax. Walt was at last back with his only son in the place where they belonged.

They ate their fish and split an Italian sub for good measure. The fire was continually fed by the supply of chopped, dry hardwood left under the canoe storage at the side of the house. The constant breeze kept the flames flickering yellow and orange as embers popped. With the fire in no danger of going out they went into the camp for another drink.

As he helped his father to his feet, Connor smiled. Despite the banged up older version of Walt in front of him, he saw the Walt he spent so much time with as a kid. All the memories came rushing back. Weekend fishing trips, evenings on the baseball diamond where Walt would hit him ground balls until neither of them could see, and nights of listening to ballgames on the radio in the car until he fell asleep. He felt his guard disappear once again, and with a glance from Walt he knew that the feeling was mutual. Connor felt he was finally back in the presence of his oldest ally, friend, mentor, and father.

It was dim inside but the propane lanterns hanging on hooks allowed them plenty of light to see the tiny card table in the center of the room. Walt sat first, gingerly, letting out a little grunt. He was in pain but knew that with a clean wound he would be all right. Hell, it would even be proof that the whole thing happened.

"My boy, reach up to your right there, and open the cupboard. On the second shelf in the back do you see a board to the left that is darker than the others?" Walt motioned.

"Yea? What's that about?" Connor inquired, intrigued by the mystery.

"Push one side of it and let it spin then pull the whole board right the hell outta there."

Connor did so without a hesitation.

"You see that bottle? That's a thirty-year old bottle

of scotch. Bring that over here would you?" Walt signaled, wincing a bit from the pain. "Grab the two glass coffee mugs. We aren't mixing this stuff and we aren't drinking outta plastic cups either."

"Macallan 18-year old sherry oak single malt scotch whiskey. Damn, that couldn't have been cheap. When did you sneak this in here? And what's up with the secret cabinet? I thought you said thirty years?" Connor asked.

"Well, as for the scotch itself, it was barrel-aged eighteen years when we bought it, your grandfather and me, about twelve years ago. The bottle has just been sitting up there since then. If we'd have left it in a barrel it would be worth a lot more now," Walt chuckled. "We got it to share with you on one of the trips down, just the three of us. We had wanted to save it for when you were in college and we hid it away as something special not to be drank by any of our friends or fellow fisherman. As the years went on it seemed there weren't really any times when it was just the three of us anymore and then after a while there wasn't all three of us at all," Walt drifted off in volume and tone.

Reeling from the thoughtfulness of his father, Connor didn't know what to say. Standing there he was a little in awe. This was almost as uncharted as being confronted with an angry bear.

"You got your letter from Papa Peter, right?" Walt continued.

"Yes, of course, that is what kicked me into gear to get back up here," Connor said, still a bit confused.

"Well I got a letter too. Mine said to basically get my ass up to camp and that I would know when to go. I didn't really know what to do with that for a few days but when you showed up I knew he wanted us up here together, like old times. In his letter he reminded me of the scotch we bought and had been saving for you. I forgot about it a few years ago and felt pretty guilty when the old man remembered and I didn't," Walt said, looking at his feet again.

"You aren't the only one feeling guilty. I can't believe I didn't go to the wake, that I let things go this far," Connor confessed.

"I am one hundred percent certain that Peter didn't want either of us to feel bad. That just wasn't his style. I raised you to be independent and strong and damn if that isn't who you are today. I may not have always done things right on the first try. Toward the end that was all he talked about with me. It's like he knew he wasn't going to be around forever and wanted to make things right, even things that he didn't make wrong." Walt paused, his gaze still downcast as his words float-ed up to both father and son. "I know I don't say it often, but I love ya kid." He said, looking up into Connor's eyes being as candid as he had possibly ever been in his son's adult life.

"You too, Dad. I'd never be who I am without you," Connor said, leaning down and hugging his seated father, careful to avoid the bandages. This was now the second hug in several years, both happening in one afternoon. With a deep breath they looked at each other as if to acknowledge the signing of peace treaty and the mending of old wounds.

"How 'bout some of that scotch bub. It's been wait-ing for us to drink it a long time now!" Walt yelled, trad-ing sentiment for triumph.

"Yes sir! Two Maccallan neat, coming up," Connor

exclaimed.

Grabbing the scotch off the dark counter and heading to the table, Connor opened the bottle and begun pouring two fingers of scotch in each mug before he noticed an envelope taped to the bottle.

"What's this? Part of the hidden cabinet scotch plan?" Connor joked with his father.

"No, I don't remember that being there," Walt looked at the bottle, surprised. "Open it up, let's see what's inside."

"Looks like a third letter! Papa Peter, never a dull moment, eh?" Connor rang out.

The two of them stopped and looked at each other for a moment. The excitement of the find was quickly grounded by the solemnity of the situation. Peter Hennessey, ever the family man, had left this letter for them to read together at the cabin and that gesture sank in for both Hennessey boys simultaneously. Opening the envelope and pulling out the white sheet of folded paper, Connor took a deep breath, then started reading aloud:

Well boys, if you've gotten to this letter than I have to assume you are both together up at camp and are enjoying one hell of a bottle of good scotch. It means the world to me that the two of you are together. There is no stronger bond than that of a father and son and I feel fortunate in my lifetime to have had two generations of Hennessey sons. Now I know things haven't always been perfect, especially these last few years, but that's life. Sometimes you just have to take a step back and look at the big picture. That can be tough for a couple of stubborn old Maine boys such as yourselves. If this letter is any indication, you should see now that life is short and the time you have together won't last forever. The river has a funny way of putting things in perspective, helping you to realize what is really important. Remember all the good times we had together? Walt you remember teaching Connor how to tie on a swivel? Connor you remember falling into the river and your father fishing you out by the seat of your pants? You have to take care of each other. It's more important than you may realize now, but someday you will see.

With that line they both looked at each other and smiled. It was almost eerie how much it rang true. Walt's expression went from acknowledgment to epiphanic bewilderment as he reached for the wound on his back. Connor realized how much he had learned from them both and that he and his father could have ended up at the bottom of the river if it hadn't been for one another. With this, they both raised a glass.

"To Peter," said Walt, stern and proud.

"To Peter," Connor echoed in return.

Nothing else needed to be said, they knew.

Connor turned his attention back to the sheet of paper. Scanning the bottom of the page he noticed something else.

Turn this letter over.

Doing so, Connor saw a 4x6 inch photo of the three of them from when he was a kid. They were on the river bank with the cabin in the background during a sunny day. They had ten brook trout all laid out on a paddle in front of them. The bottom of the paper seemed heavy and Connor realized there was something behind the photo. Carefully pulling the tape off the letter he could see two keys attached to the back of the picture. On it read:

To my boys Walt and Connor, I leave you each a key to the camp. It's yours to share and may it bring you as much happiness as it brought me for all these years. Throw my old rusty key in the river where it belongs. I hope you catch as many fish as I did up here. It may take you a lifetime but who knows, after all, fishing is in your blood. Take care of each other and keep it between the notched pines.

Hunter Nichols is an American author born and raised in central Maine who now resides in Boston, Massachusetts. He is a writer of fiction. He spends his free time exploring the great outdoors and traveling as often as possible with his wife Julia. With fishing, reading, writing and travel as his interests he traverses the globe connecting with nature and culture as frequently as possible.